SING A SONG OF PEOPLE

by Lois Lenski

Illustrated by Giles Laroche

K

D0608158

EARLY BIRD COLLECTION AUTHORS

John McInnes, *Senior Author*   Glen Dixon   John Ryckman

early bird

Okanagan College
Curriculum Resource Centre

PUBLISHED SIMULTANEOUSLY IN 1990 BY:

Nelson Canada,
A Division of International
Thomson Limited
1120 Birchmount Road
Scarborough, Ontario   M1K 5G4

AND

Delmar Publishers Inc.,
A Division of Thomson Corp.
2 Computer Drive, West
Box 15015
Albany, NY 12212-5015

**Canadian Cataloguing
in Publication Data**

Lenski, Lois, 1983-
  Sing a song of people

(Early bird collection)
ISBN 0-17-603039-5

I. Laroche, Giles. II. Title. III. Series.

PZ7.L54Si   1990   j813'.52   C89-095095-4

**Library of Congress
Cataloging-in-Publication Data**

Lenski, Lois, 1983-
  Sing a song of people.

(Early bird)
  Summary: Depicts the pleasures of city life,
people alone and in crowds, smiling and hurrying,
on the sidewalk, bus, and subway.
  [1. City and town life—Fiction. 2. Stories in
rhyme] I. Laroche, Giles, ill. II.Title.
III. Series: Early bird (Albany N.Y.)
PZ8.3.L546Si   1990   [E]   89-23352
ISBN 0-8273-4133-4

© Nelson Canada,
A Division of International Thomson Limited, 1990

All rights in this book are reserved.

Text copyright © 1965 by The Lois Lenski Covey Foundation, Inc.
Illustrations copyright © 1987 by Giles Laroche
Originally published in the United States of America by Little, Brown and Company.

Text reprinted by permission of The Lois Lenski Covey Foundation, Inc.
Illustrations reprinted by permission of Little, Brown and Company.

Co-ordinating Editor: Jean Stinson
Project Manager: Jocelyn Van Huyse-Wilson
Editor: Irene Cox
Art Director: Lorraine Tuson
Series Design and Art Direction: Rob McPhail
Typesetting: Trigraph Inc.
1 2 3 4 5 6 7 8 9 0 EB 9 8 7 6 5 4 3 2 1 0

Sing a song of people
Walking fast or slow;

People in the city,
Up and down they go.

People on the sidewalk,

People on the bus;

People passing, passing,

In back and front of us.

People on the subway
Underneath the ground;

People riding taxis
Round and round and round.

People with their hats on,

Going in the doors;

People with umbrellas
When it rains and pours.

People in tall buildings

And in stores below;

Riding in elevators,
Up and down they go.

Okanagan College
Curriculum Resource Centre

People walking singly,

People in a crowd;

People saying nothing,
People talking loud.

People laughing, smiling,

Grumpy people too;

People who just hurry
And never look at you!

Sing a song of people
Who like to come and go;

Sing of city people
You see but never know!

Okanagan College
Curriculum Resource Centre